D1685567

22055133L

CLACKMANNANSHIRE
LIBRARIES
WITHDRAWN

Oxford University Press, Walton Street, Oxford 0X2 6DP

Oxford   New York   Toronto
Delhi Bombay Calcutta Madras Karachi
Kuala Lumpur Singapore Hong Kong Tokyo
Nairobi Dar es Salaam Cape Town
Melbourne Auckland Madrid

and associated companies in
Berlin Ibadan

Oxford is a trade mark of Oxford University Press

The text of this edition is after the version by Joseph Jacobs

Copyright © Val Biro 1989
Reprinted 1990, 1992, 1993
First published in paperback 1992
Reprinted 1993
This edition first published 1994

All rights reserved

A CIP catalogue record for this book is available from the British Library

ISBN 0 19 278218 5 (hardback)
ISBN 0 19 272279 4 (paperback)

Typeset by Pentacor PLC, High Wycombe, Bucks.
Printed in Hong Kong

Jack and the Beanstalk

Val Biro

2205513L

Oxford University Press

Once upon a time there was a poor widow who had a son called Jack and a cow called Milky-white. All they had to live on was the milk from the cow. But one day Milky-white gave no more milk and the mother was in despair.

'Cheer up, Mother,' said Jack. 'We can sell the cow and then we'll see what we can do.' So he took the halter and led Milky-white off to market.

On the way he met a gnarled old man with twinkly eyes.

'Well now,' said the old man, 'you look like a smart lad. I wonder if you know how many beans make five?'

'Two in each hand and one in your mouth,' said Jack, as sharp as a needle.

'In that case,' twinkled the old man, 'here are the very beans themselves. They are magic, mind, and if you plant them overnight they'll reach the sky by morning. I'll swop them for your cow.'

Magic beans for an old cow! Now *that* was a good bargain, thought Jack, handing over Milky-white and pocketing the beans. He was sharp right enough.

'Beans?' shrieked his mother when he got home.
'Five dried-up miserable beans for a cow? You are an
idiot! Nincompoop! Dunderhead! Take that! And that!
As for your precious beans, here they go out of the
window!' She was beside herself with rage and sent
Jack to bed without any supper.

So Jack shuffled upstairs, hungry and miserable.

But when he woke next morning he stared in
amazement. His room was bathed in green light, shaded
by great big leaves right outside his window. The leaves
of a huge beanstalk that reached the sky! So the old
man had been right after all.

Jack opened the window, jumped on to the beanstalk,
and began to climb.

He climbed and
he climbed and
he climbed, until
at last he reached
the sky. And when
he got there he
found himself on a
rocky road leading
to a great big
castle.

A great big woman stood there. Jack was hungry after
his climb, so he asked her politely for some breakfast.

'Breakfast?' she boomed. 'It's breakfast you'll be if
you don't move off. My husband's an Ogre and he likes
to eat boys on toast!'

But she took pity on him, and
led him into the kitchen. Jack
wasn't halfway through his meal
when thump! thump! thump!
the castle began to shake.

'My old man's coming!'
wailed the woman and bundled
Jack into the oven.

In came the huge Ogre, sniffing.
'*Fee-fi-fo-fum,*
I smell the blood of an Englishman,
Be he alive or be he dead,
I'll grind his bones to make my bread.'

'Nonsense, dear,' said his wife, 'you're dreaming. Just
sit down and have your breakfast. You'll feel better then.'

Well, the Ogre had his breakfast, and after that he went to a chest, took out two bags of gold, sat down again and began to count. Soon he fell asleep, snoring enough to shake the rafters.

Then Jack crept out on tiptoe from his oven, put one of the bags of gold over his shoulder, and off he pelted.

He climbed down the
beanstalk, down
and down,
until at last he got home.
'Well, mother, wasn't
I right about the beans?
They *were* magical, you see!'

So they lived on the gold for some time, but at last
it ran out and Jack decided to try his luck again.

Up the beanstalk he climbed,
up and up, until he saw the
great big woman again.

'Aren't you the boy who came
here once before?' she asked. 'That
very day my Ogre missed one
of his bags of gold.'

'That's strange,' said Jack.
'I dare say I could tell you
something about that,
but I can't speak till I've had
something to eat.'

Well, the great big woman
was so curious that she took
him indoors and gave him
breakfast.

Jack had hardly finished
when thump! thump! thump!
the castle began to shake
again. 'Quick!' said the
woman and hid Jack in the
cupboard.

'*Fee-fi-fo-fum*,' said the huge Ogre sniffing around, looking very suspicious. But then he sat down to have his breakfast. After that he asked his wife to bring in the speckled hen, and she put it on the table.

'*Lay!*' said the Ogre, and the hen laid an egg all of gold.

The Ogre pocketed it, yawned and began to snore till the whole castle shook.

Jack crept out on tiptoe
from his cupboard, took the
speckled hen under his arm and
ran away. But the hen gave a cackle
and woke the Ogre who began to shout.
That was all Jack heard, because he was
off and down that beanstalk like a shot.

Well, Jack and his mother became rich, what with a golden egg every time they said 'Lay!'. But Jack was not content, and before long he determined to try his luck for a third time.

So one fine morning he climbed up the beanstalk, and he climbed and he climbed.

And when he reached the great big castle he hid behind a bush until he saw the Ogre's wife come out with a pail. Then Jack tiptoed into the castle and hid under the lid of a cauldron.

Thump! thump! thump! he heard and in came the Ogre and
his wife. *'Fee-fi-fo-fum, I smell the blood of an Englishman,'*
roared the Ogre and sniffed around the oven, the cupboard
and everything, only luckily he didn't think of the cauldron.
So he sat down to breakfast.

Then his wife brought in a golden
harp and the Ogre said *'Sing!'*
And the harp sang most beautifully
till the Ogre fell asleep.

Jack crept out on tiptoe from his cauldron, caught hold of the golden harp and dashed off towards the door. But the harp called out 'Master! Master!' and the Ogre woke up just in time to see Jack running off.

Jack ran as fast as
he could, but the Ogre came
thundering after. He would soon
have caught up, only Jack reached the
beanstalk first and started climbing down for dear life.
Just then the harp cried out: 'Master! Master!' and when
the Ogre heard this he swung himself down the beanstalk too.

By this time Jack
had climbed down
and climbed down
and climbed down
till he was very
nearly home.
But the Ogre came
down after him,
came down and
came down, and
the beanstalk was
wobbling under his
weight like a jelly.
So Jack called out:
'Mother! Mother!
Bring me an axe!'
And his mother came
rushing out with the
axe and stared in
horror to see the
Ogre's legs sticking
through the clouds.

Jack jumped down and chopped at the beanstalk with the axe. He chopped and he chopped until the beanstalk was cut in two. With a terrible cry the Ogre came tumbling down and broke his crown. There was a great big hole where he fell and the beanstalk came toppling after him. And that was that.

So what with the golden harp that sang,
the speckled hen that laid golden eggs,
and all that money, Jack and his mother
lived happily ever after.

CENTRAL REGIONAL SCHOOL LIBRARY SERVICE